Hablot Knight Browne, Julia Charlotte Maitland

The Doll and Her Friends

Memoirs of the Lady Seraphina. Fourth Edition

Hablot Knight Browne, Julia Charlotte Maitland

The Doll and Her Friends
Memoirs of the Lady Seraphina. Fourth Edition

ISBN/EAN: 9783337094195

Printed in Europe, USA, Canada, Australia, Japan

Cover: Foto ©Andreas Hilbeck / pixelio.de

More available books at **www.hansebooks.com**

THE BAZAAR.

Page 16.

THE

DOLL AND HER FRIENDS;

OR

Memoirs of the Lady Seraphina.

BY THE AUTHOR OF

"CAT AND DOG; OR, PUSS AND THE CAPTAIN,"
"HISTORICAL ACTING CHARADES,"

ETC., ETC.

WITH FOUR ILLUSTRATIONS BY HABLOT K. BROWNE.

———

Fourth Edition.

———

LONDON:
GRIFFITH AND FARRAN,
SUCCESSORS TO NEWBERY AND HARRIS,
CORNER OF ST. PAUL'S CHURCHYARD.
M.DCCC.LXII.

PREFACE.

My principal intention, or rather aim, in writing this little book was to amuse children by a story founded on one of their favourite diversions, and to inculcate a few such minor morals as my little plot might be strong enough to carry; chiefly the domestic happiness produced by kind temper and consideration for others. And further, I wished to say a word in favour of that good old-fashioned plaything, the Doll, which one now sometimes hears descried by sensible people who have no children of their own.

DOLL AND HER FRIENDS.

CHAPTER I.

I BELONG to a race the sole end of whose existence
is to give pleasure to others. None will deny the
goodness of such an end, and I flatter myself most
persons will allow that we amply fulfil it. Few of
the female sex especially but will acknowledge, with
either the smile or the sigh called forth by early
recollections, that much of their youthful happiness
was due to our presence; and some will even go so
far as to attribute to our influence many a habit of
housewifery, neatness, and industry, which ornaments their riper years.

But to our *influence*, our silent unconscious
influence alone, can such advantages be ascribed;
for neither example nor precept are in our power;
our race cannot boast of intellectual endowments;
and though there are few qualities, moral or men-
tal, that have not in their turn been imputed to us
by partial friends, truth obliges me to confess that

B

they exist rather in the minds of our admirers than in our own persons.

We are a race of mere dependants; some might even call us slaves. Unable to change our place or move hand or foot at our own pleasure, and forced to submit to every caprice of our possessors, we cannot be said to have even a will of our own. But every condition has its share of good and evil, and I have often considered my helplessness and dependence as mere trifles compared with the troubles to which poor sensitive human beings are subject.

Pain, sickness, or fatigue I never knew. While a fidgetty child cannot keep still for two minutes at a time, I sit contentedly for days together in the same attitude; and I have before now seen one of those irritable young mortals cry at a scratch, while I was bearing needles drawn in and out of every part of my body, or sitting with a pin run straight through my heart, calmly congratulating myself on being free from the inconveniences of flesh and blood.

Of negative merits I possess a good share. I am never out of humour, never impatient, never mischievous, noisy, nor intrusive; and though I and my fellows cannot lay claim to brilliant powers either in word or deed, we may boast of the same qualifications as our wittiest king, for certainly none of us ever " said a foolish thing," if she " never did a wise one."

Personal beauty I might almost, without vanity, call the " badge of all our tribe." Our very name is seldom mentioned without the epithet *pretty* ; and in my own individual case I may say, that I have always been considered pleasing and elegant, though others have surpassed me in size and grandeur.

But our most striking characteristic is our power of inspiring strong attachment. The love bestowed on us by our possessors is proof against time, familiarity, and misfortune :

> " Age cannot wither" us, " nor custom stale "
> Our " infinite variety."

With no trace of our original beauty left,—dress in tatters, complexion defaced, features undistinguishable, our very limbs mutilated, the mere wreck of our former selves,—who has not seen one of us still the delight and solace of some tender young heart ; the confidant of its fancies, and the soother of its sorrows ; preferred to all newer claimants, however high their pretensions; the still unrivalled favourite, in spite of the laughter of the nursery and the quiet contempt of the schoolroom ?

Young and gentle reader, your sympathy or

your sagacity has doubtless suggested to you my name. I am, as you guess, a DOLL; and though not a doll of any peculiar pretensions, I flatter myself that my life may not be quite without nterest to the young lovers of my race, and in this hope I venture to submit my memoirs to your indulgent consideration.

I am but a small doll; not one of those splendid specimens of wax, modelled from the Princess Royal, with distinct fingers and toes, eyes that shut, and tongues that wag. No; such I have only contemplated from a respectful distance as I lay on my stall in the bazaar, while they towered sublime in the midst of the toys, the wonder and admiration of every passing child. I am not even one of those less magnificent, but still dignified, leathern-skinned individuals, requiring clothes to take off and put on, and a cradle to sleep in, with sheets, blankets, and every thing complete. Neither can I found my claim to notice upon any thing odd or unusual in my appearance : I am not a negro doll, with wide mouth and woolly hair; nor a doll with a gutta-percha face, which can be twisted into all kinds of grimaces.

I am a simple English doll, about six inches high, with jointed limbs and an enamel face, a slim waist and upright figure, an amiable smile, an intelligent eye, and hair dressed in the first style of fashion. I never thought myself vain, but I own that in my youth I did pique myself upon my hair. There was but one opinion about *that*. I have often heard even grown-up people remark, " How ingeniously that doll's wig is put on, and how nicely it is arranged !" while at the same time my rising vanity was crushed by the insinuation that I had an absurd smirk or a ridiculous stare.

However, the opinions of human beings of mature age never much disturbed me. The world was large enough for them and me; and I could contentedly see them turn to their own objects of interest, while I awaited in calm security the unqualified praise of those whose praise alone was valuable to me—their children and grandchildren.

I first opened my eyes to the light in the Pantheon Bazaar. How I came there I know not; my conscious existence dates only from the moment in which a silver-paper covering was removed from my face, and the world burst upon my view. A feeling of importance was the first that arose in my mind. As the hand that held me turned me from side to side, I looked about. Dolls were before me, dolls behind, and dolls on each side. For a considerable time I could see nothing else. The world seemed made for dolls. But by degrees, as my powers of vision strengthened, my horizon extended, and I perceived that portions of space were allotted to many other objects. I descried, at various distances, aids to amusement in endless succession,— balls, bats, battledores, boxes, bags, and baskets; carts, cradles, and cups and saucers. I did not then know anything of the alphabet, and I cannot say that I have quite mastered it even now; but if I were learned enough, I am sure I could go from A to Z, as initial letters of the wonders with which I soon made acquaintance.

Not that I at once became aware of the uses, or even the names, of all I saw. No one took the trouble to teach me; and it was only by dint of my own intense observation that I gained any knowledge at all. I did not at first even know that I was a doll. But I made the most of opportunities, and my mind gradually expanded.

I first learned to distinguish human beings. Their powers of motion made a decided difference between them and the other surrounding objects, and naturally my attention was early turned towards the action of the shopwoman on whose stall I lived. She covered me and my companions with a large cloth every night, and restored the daylight to us in the morning. We were all perfectly helpless without her, and absolutely under her control.

At her will the largest top hummed, or was silent; the whip cracked, or lay harmlessly by the side of the horse. She moved us from place to place, and exhibited or hid us at her pleasure; but she was always so extremely careful of our health and looks, and her life seemed so entirely devoted to us and to our advantage, that I often doubted whether she was our property or we hers. Her habits varied so little from day to day, that after watching her for a reasonable time, I felt myself perfectly acquainted with *her*, and in a condition to make observations upon others of her race.

One day a lady and a little girl stopped at our stall.

" Oh, what a splendid doll!" exclaimed the child, pointing to the waxen beauty, which outshone the rest of our tribe. It was the first time I had heard the word *Doll*, though I was well acquainted with the illustrious individual to whom it was applied; and it now flashed upon my mind, with pride and pleasure, that, however insignificant in comparison, I too was a doll. But I had not time to think very deeply about my name and nature just then, as I wished to listen to the conversation of the two human beings.

" May I buy her?" said the little girl.

" Can you afford it?" asked the lady in return. " Remember your intentions for your brother."

" Perhaps I have money enough for both," answered the child. " How much does she cost ?"

" Seven shillings," said the shopwoman, taking the doll from her place, and displaying her pretty face and hands to the utmost advantage.

" I have three half-crowns," said the little girl.

" But if you spend seven shillings on the doll," answered the lady, " you will only have sixpence left for the paint-box."

" What does a paint-box cost ?" asked the child.

" We have them of all prices," replied the shopkeeper; " from sixpence to seven shillings."

The little girl examined several with great care, and stood some time in deliberation; at last she said, " I don't think Willy would like a sixpenny one."

" It would be of no use to him," answered the lady. " He draws well enough to want better colours. If you gave it to him, he would thank you and try to seem pleased, but he would not really care for it. However, he does not know that you thought of making him a birthday present, so you are at liberty to spend your money as you like."

" Would he care for a seven shilling one?" asked the little girl.

" Yes; that is exactly what he wants."

" Then he shall have it," exclaimed the good-natured little sister. "Poor dear Willy, how many more amusements I have than he!"

She bought the best paint-box, and received sixpence in change.

"Is there anything else I can shew you?" asked the shopkeeper.

"No, thank you," she replied; and turning to the elder lady, she said, "May we go home at once, Mama? It would take me a long time to choose what I shall spend my sixpence in, and I should like to give Willy his paint-box directly."

"By all means," answered the lady; "we will lose no time; and I will bring you again to spend the sixpence whenever you please."

Without one backward glance towards the beautiful doll, the child tripped away by the side of her companion, looking the brightest and happiest of her kind.

I pondered long upon this circumstance; how long I cannot say, for dolls are unable to measure time, they can only date from any particularly striking epochs. For instance, we can say, "Such an affair happened before I lost my leg;" or, "Such an event took place before my new wig was put on;" but of the intricate divisions known to mortals by the names of hours, days, months, &c., we have no idea.

However, I meditated on the kind little sister during what appeared to me a long but not tedious period, for I was gratified at gaining some insight into the qualities proper to distinguish the human race. Readiness to shew kindness, and a preference of others' interests to her own, were virtues which I easily perceived in the little girl's conduct; but one thing perplexed me sadly: I could not understand why a doll would not have answered her kind intentions as well as a paint-box; why could she not have bought the doll which she admired so much, and have given *that* to her brother.

My thoughts were still engaged with this subject when a boy approached the stall. Boys were new characters to me, and I was glad of the opportunity to observe one. He did not bestow a look on the dolls and other toys, but asked for a box of carpenter's tools. The shopkeeper dived into some hidden recess under the counter, and produced a clumsy-looking chest, the merits of which I could not discover; but the boy pronounced it to be "just the thing," and willingly paid down its price. I followed him with my eyes as he walked about with his great box under his arm, looking from side to side, till he caught sight of another boy rather younger than himself, advancing from an opposite corner.

"Why, Geoffery," exclaimed my first friend, "where have you been all this time? I have been hunting everywhere for you."

Geoffery did not immediately answer, his mouth being, as I perceived, quite full. When at last he could open his lips, he said: "Will you have a cheesecake?"

"No, thank you," replied his friend. "We must go home to dinner so soon, that you will scarcely have time to choose your things. Where *have* you been?"

"At the pastrycook's stall," answered Geoffery; "and I must go back again before I can buy any thing. I left my five shillings there to be changed."

The boys returned together to the stall, and I saw its mistress hand a small coin to Geoffrey.

"Where is the rest?" said he.

"That is your change, sir," she replied.

"Why, you don't mean that those two or three tarts and jellies cost four and sixpence!" he exclaimed, turning as red as the rosiest doll at my side.

"I think you will find it correct, sir," answered the shopkeeper. "Two jellies, sixpence each, make one shilling; two custards, sixpence each, two shillings; a bottle of ginger-beer, threepence, two and threepence; one raspberry cream, sixpence, two and ninepence; three gooseberry tarts, threepence, three shillings; two strawberry tarts, three and twopence; two raspberry ditto, three and fourpence; four cheesecakes, three and eightpence; two Bath buns, four shillings; and one lemon ice, four and sixpence."

"What a bother!" said Geoffery, as he pocketed the small remains of his fortune. "I wish I could give her some of the tarts back again, for they weren't half so nice as they looked, except just the first one or two."

"Because you were only hungry for the first one or two," said the other boy. "But it can't be helped now; come and spend the sixpence better."

"There won't be anything worth buying for sixpence," said Geoffrey, gloomily, as he shuffled in a lazy manner towards my stall.

"I want a spade," said he.

Several were produced, but they cost two shillings or half-a-crown. There were little wooden spades for sixpence; but from those he turned with contempt, saying they were only fit for babies. Nothing at our table suited him, and he walked towards our opposite neighbour, who sold books, maps, &c. On his asking for a dissected map, all the countries of the world were speedily offered to his choice: but alas! the price was again the obstacle. The cheapest map was half-a-crown; and

Geoffrey's sixpence would buy nothing but a childish puzzle of Old Mother Hubbard. Geoffrey said it was a great shame that every thing should be either dear or stupid.

"Can't you lend me some money, Ned?" continued he.

"I can't indeed," replied the other; "mine all went in this box of tools. Suppose you don't spend the sixpence at all now, but keep it till you get some more."

"No, I won't do that; I hate saving my money."

So saying, he wandered from stall to stall, asking the price of every thing, as if his purse was as full as his stomach.

"How much is that sailor kite?" "Two shillings, sir."—"How much is that bat?" "Seven and sixpence."—"How much is that wooden box with a secret drawer?" "Three shillings."

"How provoking!" he exclaimed. "I want heaps of things, and this stupid sixpence is no good at all."

"It is better than nothing," said Edward. "It is not every day that one's aunt sends one five shillings to spend in the bazaar; and in common times sixpence is not to be despised. After all, there are plenty of things it will buy. Do you want a top?"

"No; I've got four."

" Garden seeds ?"

" What is the use of them, when I can't get a spade ?"

" Steel pens ? You said this morning you could not write with quills."

" I don't like buying those kind of things with my own money."

" A box ? Yesterday you wanted a box."

" I don't care for boxes that won't lock, and I can't get one with a lock and key for sixpence."

" A knife ?"

" Sixpenny knives have only one blade; I want two."

" Sealing-wax ? wafers ? a penholder ? a paint-box ? India-rubber ? pencils ?"

" Stupid things !"

" A ball ? You might have a very good ball."

" Not a cricket-ball; and I don't care for any other."

" What a particular fellow you are ! I am sure I could always find something to spend sixpence in. String ? One is always wanting string. You may have a good ball of whipcord."

" These sort of places don't sell it."

" Then, I say again, keep your money till you want it."

" No, that I'll never do, when I came on purpose to spend it. After all, the only thing I can think of," continued Geoffrey, after a pause, "is to go back to the pastrycook's. There was one kind of tart I did not taste, and perhaps it would be nicer than the others. I'll give you one if you like."

"No, thank you; I am much obliged to you all the same; but I won't help you to spend your money in that way. Don't buy any more tarts. Come and walk about; there are plenty more shops to look at."

They sauntered on, but Geoffrey, by various turns, worked his way back to the pastrycook's; and as no persuasions could then bring him away, Edward walked off, not choosing, as he said, to encourage him.

Presently I saw a tall gentleman enter the bazaar, and I wondered what he would buy. I did not then understand the difference between grown-up people and children, and as he approached my stall, I could not repress a hope that he would buy *me*. But his quick eye glanced over the tables without resting on any of the toys.

"Can I shew you anything, sir?" said my mistress.

"No, I am much obliged to you," he answered, with a pleasant smile. "I am only in search of some young people, who, I dare say, have been better customers than I. Ah, here they are," he continued, as the two boys of whom I had taken so much notice ran up to him from different ends of the room.

"Well, boys," said he, "what have you bought? Must we hire a waggon to carry your property home?"

"Not quite," answered Edward. "I have bought a wagon-load of amusement, but I can carry it home well enough myself; I have spent all my money in this box of tools."

"A very sensible and useful purchase," said the gentleman; "they will give you plenty of pleasant employment. The only objection is, that they are likely to be lost or broken at school."

"I do not mean to take them to school, Papa, I shall use them in the holidays, and leave them with Willy when I go back to school; that was one reason why I bought them. Willy could do a good deal of carpentering on his sofa."

"True, my boy, and a kind thought. They will be a great amusement to poor Willy, and he will take good care of them for you."

"Now, Geoffrey, how have you invested your capital? I hope you have found a strong spade. It is fine weather for gardening."

"No, I haven't," stammered Geoffrey.

" Well, what have you bought ?"

" I don't know," said Geoffrey.

" Do you mean that you have not spent your money yet ? Make haste, then, for I can only allow you five minutes more. I expected to find you ready to go home. Be brisk ; there is every thing on that stall that the heart of boy can wish," said the gentleman, pointing to my abode.

But Geoffrey did not move. " I don't want any thing," said he at last.

" What a fortunate boy !' said the gentleman ; but he presently added, " Have you lost your money ?"

" No."

" Shew it to me."

Geoffrey slowly produced his sixpence, almost hidden in the palm of his hand.

" Where is the rest ?" asked the gentleman. " Have you spent it ?"

" Yes."

" And nothing to shew for it ? Nothing ?"— and the gentleman looked at the boy more narrowly. " Nothing," said he again, " except a few crumbs of pie-crust on your waistcoat ? Oh, Geoffrey !"

There was a short silence, and the boy coloured a good deal; at last he said, " It was my own money."

c

" You will wish it was your own again before long, I dare say," said the gentleman. " However, we must hope you will be wiser in time. Come home now to dinner."

" I don't want any dinner," said Geoffrey.

" Probably not, but Edward and I do. We have not dined on tarts ; and I dare say Ned is as hungry as I am."

So saying, he led the way towards the door, leaving me, as usual, pondering over what had passed. One word used by the gentleman made a great impression on me—USEFUL.

What could that mean ? Various considerations were suggested by the question. Some things, it seemed, were useful, others not ; and what puzzled me most was, that the very same things appeared to be useful to some people, and not to others. For instance, the sixpenny paint-box, which had been rejected as useless to Willy, was bought soon afterwards by a small boy, who said it would be the most useful toy he had.

Could this be the case with every thing ? Was it possible that every thing properly applied might have its use, and that its value depended upon those who used it ? If so, why was Geoffrey blamed for spending his money in tarts? *He* liked them. Perhaps he had plenty of food at home, and that uselessness consisted in a thing's not being really wanted. I revolved the subject in my mind, and tried to discover the use of every thing I saw, but I was not always successful. The subject was perplexing; and gradually all my thoughts became fixed on the point of most importance to myself—namely, my own use.

How changed were my ideas since the time when I imagined the world to belong to dolls! Their whole race now seemed to be of very small importance; and as for my individual self, I could not be sure that I had any use at all, and still less *what*, or to *whom*.

Day after day I lay on my counter unnoticed, except by the shopwoman who covered us up at night, and re-arranged us in the morning; and even this she did with such an indifferent air, that I could not flatter myself I was of the smallest use to *her*. Every necessary care was bestowed upon me in common with my companions; but I sighed for the tender attentions that I sometimes saw lavished by children upon their dolls, and wished that my mistress would nurse and caress me in the same manner.

She never seemed to think of such a thing. She once said I was dusty, and whisked a brush over my face; but that was the only separate mark of interest I ever received from her. I had no reasonable ground of complaint, but I began to grow weary of the insipidity of my life, and to ask myself whether this could be my only destiny. Was I never to be of use to any body? From time to time other toys were carried away. Many a giddy top and lively ball left my side in childish company and disappeared through those mysterious gates by which the busy human race entered our calm seclusion.

At last even dolls had their day. The beautiful waxen princess no longer graced our dominions. She was bought by an elderly lady for a birthday present to a little grand-daughter; and on the very same day the "old familiar faces" of six dolls who had long shared my counter vanished from my sight, one after another being bought and carried away.

I was sorry to lose them, though while we lived together we had had our little miffs and jealousies. I had sometimes thought that the one with the red shoes was always sticking out her toes; that she of the flaxen ringlets was ready to let every breath of wind blow them over her neighbours' faces; that another with long legs took up more room than her share, much to my inconvenience. But now that they were all gone, and I never could hope to see

them again, I would gladly have squeezed myself
into as small compass as the baby doll in the
walnut-shell, in order to make room for them once
more.

One thing, however, was satisfactory: dolls
certainly had their use. Seven had been bought,
and therefore why not an eighth? I had been
sinking almost into a state of despondency, but
now my hopes revived and my spirits rose. My
turn might come.

And my turn did come. Every circumstance of
that eventful day is deeply impressed on my me-
mory. I was as usual employed in making remarks
upon the passing crowd, and wondering what might
be the use of every body I saw, when I perceived
the lady and the little girl who had been almost my
first acquaintances among the human race. As they
approached my stall, I heard the Mama say, "Have
you decided what to buy with the sixpence?"   .

"Oh, yes, quite," answered the child; "I am
going to buy a *sixpenny doll.*"

The words thrilled through me; her eyes seemed
fixed on mine, and the sixpence was between her
fingers. I imagined myself bought. But she continued: "I think, if you don't mind the trouble, I
should like to go round the bazaar first, to see
which are the prettiest."

"By all means," replied the lady; and they walked on, carrying all my hopes with them.

I had often fancied myself the prettiest doll of my size in the place; but such conceit would not support me now. I felt that there were dozens, nay scores, who more than equalled me; and all discontented notions of my neglected merit now sunk before the dread that I had really no merit to neglect.

I began also to have some idea of what was meant by time. My past life had glided away so imperceptibly, that I did not know whether it had been long or short; but I learnt to count every moment while those two mortals were walking round the bazaar.

I strained my eyes to catch sight of them again; but when at last they re-appeared, I scarcely dared to look, for fear of seeing a doll in the child's hands. But no; her hands were empty, except for the sixpence still between her finger and thumb.

They came nearer—they stopped at another stall; I could not hear what they said, but they turned away, and once more stood opposite to me. The child remained for some moments as silent as myself, and then exclaimed, "After all, Mama, I don't think there are any prettier dolls than these in the whole room."

" What do you say to this one, Miss ?" said our proprietor, taking up a great full-dressed Dutch doll, and laying her on the top of those of my size and class, completely hiding the poor little victims under her stiff muslin and broad ribbons.

But on the child's answering, " No, thank you, I only want a sixpenny doll not dressed," the Dutch giantess was removed, and we once more asserted our humble claims.

"That seems to me a very pretty one," said the Mama, pointing to my next neighbour. The child for a moment hesitated, but presently exclaimed in a joyful tone, " Oh, no, *this* is the beauty of all; this little darling with the real hair and blue ribbons in it; I will take this one if you please." And before I could be sure that she meant me, I was removed from my place, wrapped up in paper, and consigned to her hands. My long-cherished wishes were fulfilled, and I was bought. At first I could scarcely believe it. Notwithstanding all my planning and looking forward to this event, now that it really happened, I could not understand it. My senses seemed gone. What had so long occupied my mind was the work of a moment; but that moment was irrevocable, and my fate was decided. In my little mistress' hands I passed the boundaries of the world of toys, and entered upon a new state of existence.

CHAPTER II.

A VERY different life now opened before me. I had
no longer any pretence for complaining of neglect.
My young mistress devoted every spare moment to
the enjoyment of my company, and set no limits to
her caresses and compliments; while I in return
regarded her with all the gratitude and affection
which a doll can feel. My faculties as well as my
feelings were called into fresh exercise; for though
I had no longer the wide range of observation
afforded by the daily crowd of strangers in the
bazaar, I had the new advantage of making intimate acquaintance with a small circle of friends.

Having hitherto been so completely without any
position in the world, I could not at first help feeling rather shy at the idea of taking my place as
member of a family; and it was therefore a relief
to find that my lot was not cast amongst total
strangers, but that I had already some slight clue
to the characters of my future companions.

My mistress, whose name was Rose, was sister
to the Willy for whom she had bought the paint-
box, and also to Edward, the purchaser of the

tools.   Geoffrey, the lover of tarts, was a cousin on
a visit to them for the holidays ; and they had also
an elder sister named Margaret, besides their Papa
and Mama, whom I had seen in the bazaar.

The first of the family to whom I was introduced
was Willy, and I soon became much interested in
him.   He was a pale thin boy, who spent the day
on a sofa, to and from which he was carried in the
morning and at night. In fine weather he went
out in a wheel-chair ; but he was unable to move
without help, and was obliged to endure many priva-
tions. Though he often looked suffering and weary,
he was cheerful and patient, and always seemed
pleased to hear other children describe enjoyments
in which he could not share. Every body was fond
of Willy, and anxious to amuse and comfort him.
All that happened out of doors was told to him ; all
the kindest friends and pleasantest visitors came to
see him ; the new books were brought to him to read
first ; the best fruit and flowers always set apart for
him ; and all the in-door occupations arranged as
much as possible with a view to his convenience.
He and his little sister Rose were the dearest friends
in the world, and certain to take part in whatever
interested each other.   As soon as Rose brought
me home from the Pantheon, she ran upstairs with
me to Willy, whom I then saw for the first time,

sitting on a sofa with his feet up, and a table before him, on which stood several books, and my old acquaintances the paint-box and the chest of tools.

" Look at this, Willy; is not this pretty ? " exclaimed Rose, laying me down on his open book.

Willy looked up with a pleasant smile: " Very pretty," he answered. " I suppose she is to be the lady of the new house; and with Ned's tools I hope to make some furniture worth her acceptance."

" Oh, thank you, Willy dear. And will you help me to choose a name for her ? What do you think the prettiest name you know.

" *Rose*," answered Willy laughing ; " but I suppose that will not do. I dare say you want something very fine and out-of-the-way."

" As fine as can be," replied Rose ; " I have been thinking of Seraphina or Wilhelmina: which do you like best ?

" Call it Molly," cried Edward, who just then entered the room; " Molly and Betty are the best names : no nonsense in them."

" Call it Stupid Donkey," mumbled a voice behind him ; and Geoffrey advanced, his mouth as usual full of something besides words. " Have any nuts, Willy ? " he asked, holding out a handful.

" No, thank you," answered Willy ; " I must not eat them."

"I wouldn't be you, I know," said Geoffrey, cracking one between his teeth: "never let to eat anything but what's wholesome, and always reading, or doing something stupid. I believe you are helping Rose to play with that doll now. Put it into the fire; that is the way to treat dolls. Stupid things. I hate 'em!"

"Pray do not touch it, Geoffrey," said Rose.

"Leave it alone, Geff," said Edward. "You have your things, and Rose has hers. I don't see the fun of dolls myself, but she does, and nobody shall interfere with her while I am here to protect her. Just remember that, will you?"

"The d-o-ll!" said Geoffrey, drawling the word, and making a face as if the pronouncing it turned him quite sick. "Oh, the sweet doll! Perhaps you would like to stay and play with Rose, and Willy, and the d-o-ll, instead of coming out to cricket."

"Nonsense, you foolish fellow, you know better," answered Edward. "But I wont have Rose bullied; and what's more, I won't have Willy quizzed. I should like to see you or me pass such an examination as Willy could if he were at school. Why, he can learn as much in a day as we do in a week."

"Well, he is welcome to learn as much as he

likes," said Geoffrey; "and let's you and I go and play. What stupid nuts these are! I've almost cracked one of my teeth with cracking them."

The boys ran off; and presently there came into the room the Papa and Mama, whom I already knew and a young lady very like Rose, but older. I found she was Margaret, the eldest sister. They inquired whether Willy wanted any thing before they went out; and Margaret fetched a drawing that he wished to copy, while his father and mother wheeled his sofa and table nearer the window, that he might have more light. When he was made quite comfortable, they told Rose that she might stay and take care of him till they returned; and she said she would bring her box of scraps and begin dressing me. Then I came in for my share of notice, and had every reason to be satisfied with the praises bestowed on me. The Mama said that I deserved very neatly made clothes; the papa, that my hair would be a pattern for Margaret's; and Margaret said I was charming, and that she would make me a pink satin gown.

They admired the name *Seraphina*, though the papa suggested various others which he thought might suit Rose's taste,—Sophonisba, Cleopatra, Araminta, Dulcinea, Ethelinda, &c.; but as she remained steady to her first choice, the LADY

SERAPHINA was decided to be thenceforth my name and title.

And now began the real business of my life. I was no longer doomed to fret at being of no use, for the object of my existence was plain enough, namely, to give innocent recreation to my young mistress when at leisure from her more serious employments. Every day she spent some hours in study with her mother or sister ; and she would fly to me for relief between her lessons, and return to them with more vigour after passing a little time in my refreshing company. She often shewed her tasks to me, and discussed their difficulties. I think she repeated the multiplication-table to me nearly a hundred times, while I sat on the *Tutor's Assistant* waiting for the recurrence of the fatal words, " Seven times nine." Day after day she could get no farther ; but as soon as she came to " Seven times nine," I was turned off the book, which had to be consulted for the answer.

At last, one day she came running into the room, in great glee, exclaiming, " I have done the multiplication-table. I have said it quite right, sixty-three and all. I made no mistake even in dodging. And *you* helped me, my darling Lady Seraphina. I never could have learned it perfect if you had not heard me say it so often. And now, look at your

rewards. Margaret has made you a bonnet, and
Willy has made you an arm-chair."

Beautiful, indeed, was the bonnet, and commo-
dious the arm-chair; and I wore the one and re-
clined in the other all the time Rose was learning
the French auxiliary verbs *être* and *avoir*. I flat-
tered myself I was of as much use in them as in the
multiplication-table; but I do not recollect receiving any particular recompense. Indeed, after a little
time, it would have been difficult to know what to
give me, for I possessed everything that a doll's
heart could wish, or her head imagine. Such a
variety of elegant dresses as Rose made for me
would have been the envy of all my old friends in
the bazaar. I had gowns of pink satin and white
satin; blue silk and yellow silk; coloured muslins
without number, and splendid white lace. Bonnets
enough to furnish a milliner's shop were mine; but
I was not so partial to them as to my gowns, because they tumbled my hair.

I believe a good many of my possessions were
presents from Margaret to Rose on account of
perfect lessons; but in course of time, I ceased
to superintend Rose's studies. Margaret said
that I interrupted the course of history; and
the Mama said that Rose was old enough to
learn her lessons without bringing her play into

them, and that I must be put away during school hours.

Though I did not think that the fault was altogether mine, I quite acquiesced in the wisdom of this decree; for during Rose's last reading-lesson she had stopped so often to ask me which I liked best, Lycurgus or Solon, Pericles or Alcibiades, &c., that Margaret was almost out of patience. And though I made no answer, and had really no choice at all between the characters, I felt that I rather hindered business.

I was therefore now left to myself for several hours in the morning; but I found ample and pleasant employment in surveying the comforts and beauties of my habitation. For I was not forced to perform the part of an insignificant pigmy in the vast abodes of the colossal race of man : I possessed a beautiful little house proportioned to my size, pleasantly situated on a table in the furthest corner of the school-room, and commanding an extensive view of the whole apartment.

I must describe my house at full length. It had been originally, as I heard, a mere rough packing case; but what of that? The best brick house in London was once but clay in the fields; and my packing-case was now painted outside and papered inside, and fitted up in a manner every

way suitable for the occupation of a doll of dis-
tinction.

My drawing-room was charming; light and
cheerful, the walls papered with white and gold,
and the floor covered with a drab carpet worked
with flowers of every hue. Rose worked the carpet
herself under the directions of Margaret, who pre-
vailed on her to learn worsted-work for my sake.
So there, again, how useful I was!   From the ceiling hung a brilliant glass chandelier, a birthday
present from Edward to Rose; and the mantelpiece
was adorned by a splendid mirror cut out of a
broken looking-glass by Willy, and framed by his
hands. I cannot say that Willy ever seemed to care
for me personally, but he took considerable interest
in my upholstery, and much of my handsomest
furniture was manufactured by him.   He made my
dining-room and drawing-room tables; the frames
of my chairs, which were covered with silk by Margaret; my sofa and my four-post bedstead; and it
was he who painted the floor-cloth in my hall, and
the capital picture of the Queen and Prince Albert
which hung over the dining-room chimney-piece. I
had a snug bed-room, containing a bed with pink
curtains, a toilette-table, with a handsome looking-
glass, pin-cushion, and rather large brush and comb;
a washing-stand, towel-horse, chest of drawers, and

wardrobe. But the last two, I must confess, were rather for show than for use. They were French-polished, and in appearance convenient as well as handsome, but in reality too small to hold my clothes. A few minor articles of dress were kept in them; but the mass of my gorgeous attire was always in larger boxes and trunks belonging to my mistress; her work-box, for instance, and at one time her desk; but her Mama turned all my gowns out of the latter when she banished me from the lessons, and desired that, for the future, only writing materials should be kept in it. "Every thing in its proper place, Rose," I heard her say. "You have plenty of little boxes for doll's clothes; and your doll ought to teach you to be more tidy instead of less so."

My dining-room was well adapted for all the purposes of hospitality, being furnished with a substantial dining-table, chairs, and a sideboard, on which there always stood two trays, one filled with decanters and wine-glasses, and the other with knives and forks.

My kitchen was resplendent with saucepans, kettles, pots and pans, and plates and dishes, ranged upon the dresser, or hung from the walls. A joint of meat was always roasting before the fire, and a cook of my own race appeared to spend her life in basting it, for I never failed to find her thus employed when Rose was so kind as to take me into my kitchen. There was also a footman, who sat for ever in the hall; and I was inclined to consider him rather wanting in respect, till I discovered that, owing to a broken leg, he was unable to stand. I did not quite comprehend the use of my servants, as Rose herself did all the work of my house; but she said they were indispensable, and that if it were not for want of room, I should have a great many more.

Besides all these arrangements for my comfort in-doors, I possessed a beautiful open phaeton, emblazoned with the royal arms of England, and drawn by four piebald horses with long tails, so spirited that they never left off prancing. Every day, after school-time, Rose brought this equipage to my door; and the four horses stood with their eight front feet in the air while I was dressed for my drive. Then, attired in my last new bonnet and cloak, I sat in state in my carriage, and was drawn round and round the room by Rose, till she said I was tired. She made many attempts to persuade the lame footman to stand on the footboard behind, but she never could manage it. He was a very helpless creature; and I am not quite certain that he even did his best, little as that might be.

The first time Rose set him up behind the carriage, he tumbled head over heels into the middle of it, and stood there on his head till she picked him out again. Then he fell off behind, then on one side, and then on the other, till she was quite tired of his foolish tricks, and left him to sit quietly and stupidly in his old place in the hall.

I lived in great comfort in my pleasant house, and being of a cheerful, contented temper, never felt lonely, although left to myself during great part of the day; for Rose was very obedient to her Mama's orders, and even if now and then tempted to forget the regulation herself, Willy was always at hand to remind her, and help to fix her attention on her business. But when it was all over, she flew to me with redoubled pleasure.

One day she said to me, " My dear Seraphina, I am afraid you must be very dull, alone all the morning." I longed to assure her of the contrary; but not having the gift of speech, I could only listen submissively while she continued: " It is a pity that you should sit doing nothing and wasting your time; so I have brought you some books, which you are to read while I am at my lesson; and I shall expect you to learn just as much as I do."

So saying, she seated me on my sofa, and

placing a table with the books before me, " Look,"
continued she, " I have made them for you myself,
and covered them with these pretty red and green
papers.   This is your English History, and this is
your French Grammar; and here is a Geography
Book, and here is a History of Rome.   Now read
attentively, and do not let your thoughts wander ;
and be very careful not to dogs-ear the leaves ; that
always looks like a dunce.   And mind you sit upright," added she, looking back, as she left the room
in obedience to a summons from her sister.

I obeyed to the best of my power.   To be sure,
I did not know which was geography and which was
grammar;   and English and Roman History were
both alike to me.   But I did as I was bid.   I sat
upright in the place appointed me, staring as hard
as I could at the open pages; and my worst enemy
could not accuse me of dogs-earing a single leaf.

When my mistress returned, she pleased me
much by calling me a very good girl, and saying
that if I continued to take so much pains, I could
not fail to improve.   On hearing this, Willy
laughed, and said he hoped that that was a duplicate of Margaret's last speech ; and Rose looked
very happy, and answered that not only Margaret,
but Mama had said the same.

This was not my only duplicate of Rose's adventures. My education appeared to be conducted precisely on the same plan as her own. Before long, she brought a little pianoforte and set it up in my drawing-room. I thought it rather hid the pretty paper, but it was a handsome piece of furniture.

"Now, Lady Seraphina," said Rose, "I am obliged to practise for an hour every day, and you must do the same. See what a pretty piano I have given you. You need not mind its being meant for a housewife and pincushion; the notes are marked, and that is all you want. Now practise your scales, and be very careful to play right notes and count your time."

I sat at my piano with all due diligence, but I am sorry to say that my progress did not seem satisfactory. One day Rose said that she was sure I had forgotten to count; and another day, that I hurried the easy bars and slackened the difficult ones; then she accused me of not caring whether I played right notes or wrong, and torturing her ear by my false chords; then I banged the notes till I broke the strings: in short, there was no end to her complaints, till at last she wound them all up by declaring that both she and I hated music, and that if Mama and Margaret would take her advice, we should both leave it off.

But still I practised regularly, and so, I suppose, did Rose; and gradually her reproaches diminished, and she grew more contented with me; and we both persevered, till she said that really, after all, I seemed to have a good ear, and to be likely to make a very respectable player.

"But you know it all depends upon yourself, Seraphina; your present improvement is the result of pains and practice. Pains and practice will do any thing."

It was fortunate for me that I had so careful a superintendent as Rose; for unless she had kept a constant watch over me, there is no saying how many awkward habits I might unconsciously have contracted. But she cured me of poking my head forward, of standing on one leg, of tilting my chair, of meddling with things that were not my own, of leaning against the furniture while I was speaking, of putting my elbows on the table, of biting my nails, of spilling my tea, and of making crumbs on the floor.

I cannot say I was myself aware either of the faults or their cure; but I think one seldom does notice one's own faults, and therefore it is a great advantage to have kind friends who will point them out to us. I believed Rose when she told me of mine; so I had a right to believe her when she gave me the agreeable assurance of their cure, and to indulge the hope that I was becoming a pleasing, well-bred little doll.

On one mortifying occasion, however, I must own that Rose's anxiety for my always following in her steps was the cause of a serious injury to me. She remarked that I had got into a horrid way of kicking off my shoes while I was learning my poetry; and she thought the best cure would be to make me wear sandals. I observed that she was sewing sandals to her own shoes at the time, and she consulted Willy about some means of doing the same by mine. Willy held me head downwards, and examined my feet. My shoes were painted, therefore sewing was out of the question. He advised glue. This was tried, but it came through the thin narrow ribbon of which my sandals were to be made, and looked very dirty. They were taken off; but the operation had spoilt the delicacy of my white stockings, and Rose said it was impossible to let me go such an untidy figure; we must try some other way. She asked Willy to lend her a gimlet, that she might bore holes at the sides of my feet, and glue the ribbon into them, so as not to shew the glue. Willy said she was welcome to the gimlet, but that he advised her to leave it alone, for that she would only break my feet. But Rose would not be dissuaded, and began boring.

It was on this occasion that I most peculiarly felt the advantage of that insensibility to pain which distinguishes my race. What mortal could have borne such an infliction without struggling and screaming? I, on the contrary, took it all in good part, and shewed no signs of feeling even at the fatal moment when my foot snapped in two; and Rose, with a face of utter dismay, held up my own toes before my eyes.

"Oh, my poor Seraphina!" she exclaimed, "what shall we do?"

"Glue it on again," said Willy. "You had better have taken my advice at first, but now you must make the best of it. Glue is your only friend."

So Rose glued the halves of my foot together, lamenting over me, and blaming herself so much all the time, that it seemed rather a comfort to her when Margaret, coming into the room, agreed with her that she had been foolish and awkward. Margaret said that ribbon might have been tied over my feet from the first, without using glue or gimlet either; and Rose called herself more stupid than ever, for not having thought of such an easy contrivance.

My foot was glued, and for the purpose of standing, answered as well as ever; and Rose sewed me up in a pair of blue silk boots, and declared that I was prettier than before; and my misfortune was soon forgotten by every body but myself. I, however, could not but feel a misgiving that this was the first warning of my share in the invariable fate of my race. For I had already lived long enough to be aware that the existence of a doll, like that of every thing else, has its limits. Either by sudden accidents, such as loss of limbs, or by the daily wear and tear of life, decay gradually makes its progress in us, and we fade away as surely as the most delicate of the fragile race of mortals.

Though the fracture of my foot was my own first misfortune, I had had opportunities of remarking the casualties to which dolls are liable. For it is not to be supposed that our devotion to human beings precludes us from cultivating the society of our own species. Dolls will be dolls; and they have a natural sympathy with each other, notwithstanding the companionship of the race of man. Most little girls are aware of this fact, and provide suitable society for their dolls. I myself had a large circle of silent acquaintances, to whom I was introduced by Rose's kindness and consideration. When other little girls came to drink tea with her, they often brought their dolls to spend the evening with me; and among them I had more than once the pleasure of recognizing an old friend from the bazaar.

Then I was in my glory. There was a constant supply of provisions in my larder; and at a moment's notice Rose would produce an excellent dinner, all ready cooked, and dished in a beautiful little china dinner-service. Willy compared her to the genius of Aladdin's lamp; and though I did not know what that might mean, I quite understood the advantage of being able to set such a banquet before my friends. I could always command salmon, a pair of soles, a leg of mutton, a leg of pork, a turkey, a pair of boiled fowls, a ham, a sucking pig, a hare, a loaf of bread, a fine Cheshire cheese, several pies, and a great variety of fruit, which was always ripe and in season, winter or summer. Rose's papa once observed that his hothouse produced none so fine; for the currants were as large as apples, and two cherries filled a dish.

Rose and her companions performed the active duties of waiting at table on these occasions; but the lame footman was generally brought out of the hall, and propped up against the sideboard, where he stood looking respectable but awkward.

At these pleasant parties I saw a great range of characters, for Rose's young visitors were various in their tastes, and their dolls used to be dressed in every known costume. Besides plenty of pretty English damsels, I was introduced now to a Turkish

THE DOLL'S PARTY.

Page 42

sultana, now to a Swiss peasant; one day to a captain in the British army, another day to an Indian rajah. One young lady liked to make her dolls personate celebrated characters; and when she visited us, most distinguished guests graced my table. I have had the honour of receiving the Queen and Prince Albert themselves; the Duke of Wellington, Sir Walter Scott, and Miss Edgeworth, have all dined with me on the same day, and Robinson Crusoe came in the evening.

But it was at these social meetings that I became most fully aware of the liability of dolls to loss of limbs. I never remember giving a party at which the guests could boast of possessing all their legs and arms. Many an ingenious contrivance hid or supplied the deficiencies, and we were happy in spite of our losses; still, such was the case: and I saw that dolls, however beloved and respected, could not last for ever.

For some time after my accident I had no particular adventures. I lived in peace and plenty, and amused myself with watching the family. They were all amiable and easy to understand, except Geoffrey; but he was a complete puzzle to me, and it was long before I could make out why he was so different from the rest.

The others all seemed to like to help and please

one another, but Geoffrey never seemed happy unless he was making himself disagreeable. If Willy was interested in a book, he was obliged to sit upon the second volume, or Geoffrey would be sure to run away with it. If Edward was in a hurry to go out, Geoffrey would hide his cap, and keep him a quarter of an hour hunting for it. The girls dared not leave their worsted-work within his reach for a moment; for he would unravel the canvass, or chop up the wool, or go on with the work after a pattern of his own composing, so that they would be obliged to spend half an hour in unpicking his cobbling.

Margaret remonstrated with him in private, and made excuses for him in public, and did her best to prevent his tiresome tricks from annoying Willy ; Edward tried rougher means of keeping him in order, which sometimes succeeded; but still he could find plenty of opportunities of being a torment: people always can when such is their taste.

One day Margaret was keeping Willy company, while the rest of the party were gone to the Zoological Gardens. She had brought a drawing to finish, as he liked to see her draw, and was sometimes useful in suggesting improvements. But while they were thus employed, Margaret was summoned to some visitors, and went away, saying that her drawing would just have time to dry before she returned.

But unfortunately, during her absence, Geoffrey came home. He had grown tired of the gardens, which he had seen very often, and rather hungry, as he generally was; so after amusing himself by eating the cakes he had bought for the bear, he had nothing more to do, and tried to persuade his cousins to be tired also. But Edward was making himself agreeable to the monkeys, Rose was cultivating the friendship of the elephant, and their Papa and Mama were waiting to see the hippopotamus bathe; so that Geoffrey's proposals of leaving the Gardens were scouted, and he could only obtain leave from his uncle to go home by himself.

He entered the room, as usual, with his mouth full, having spent his last penny in a peace of cocoanut as he came along the streets. While the cocoanut lasted, he was employed to his satisfaction; but when that was finished, he was again at a loss for something to do. He tried walking round the room on one leg, working heel and toe, and that succeeded very well, and did no harm till he unluckily came to the drawing-table, when he immediately brought himself to a stand on both feet.

"Hallo!" cried he, "here's a daub! Is this your splendid performance, Will?"

"No," replied Willy, "it is Margaret's; and mind you don't touch it by accident, because it is wet."

"Touch it by accident!" exclaimed Geoffrey; "I am going to touch it on purpose. I wonder Margaret is not ashamed to do it so badly. I'll improve it for her. How kind of me!"

Poor Willy, in dismay, tried to secure the drawing, but he could not move from his sofa, and Geoffrey danced round him, holding it at arm's-length. Then Willy caught at the bell-rope, but his mischievous cousin snatched it quicker, and tied it up out of his reach. Willy called all the servants as loud as he could, but no one was within hearing; and he threw himself back on his sofa in despair, exclaiming, "How can you be so ill-natured, when Margaret is always so kind to you?"

"Ill-natured!" answered the other; "I'am doing her a favour. She admired the moonlight in the Diorama; now I shall make just such a moon in her drawing." And while he spoke, a great yellow moon, like a guinea, rose in the midst of poor Margaret's brilliant sunset.

"That's the thing," said Geoffrey; "and now I shall put the cow jumping over it, and the little dog laughing to see such sport. Some figures always improve the foreground.

"Oh, you have quite spoilt it!" cried Willy.

"How I wish I could stop you! I cannot imagine how you can like to be so mischievous and disagreeable. Oh, if Margaret would but come back!"

At last Margaret came, and the troublesome Geoffrey expected great amusement from her displeasure; but he was disappointed. Margaret was one of those generous people who never resent an injury done to themselves. If Geoffrey had spoilt any body else's drawing, she would have been the first to punish him; but now she was much more vexed at Willy's distress than at the destruction of her own work, and instead of scolding Geoffrey, she gave herself up to consoling Willy. She assured him that there was no great harm done. She said the drawing was good for very little, and that she would copy it and improve it so much that he should be quite glad of the disaster; and she made a present of the spoilt drawing to Geoffrey, telling him she was sure he would one day be ashamed of so foolish a performance, but that meanwhile he might keep it as a specimen of his taste. He had not the manners to apologise, but he looked very silly and crest-fallen, and left the room in silence, with the drawing in his hand.

When he was gone, Willy exclaimed, "If it were not for losing Edward, I should wish the holidays were over; Geoffrey is so disagreeable."

"He is very thoughtless," Margaret replied; "but we must not be too hard upon him. Let us recollect that he has no parents to teach him better, nor brothers and sisters to call forth his consideration for others. Poor Geoffrey has had neither example nor precept till now. But now Papa and Mama give him good precepts; and if we try to set him good examples, perhaps we may help him to improve."

"Well, I'll hope for the best, and do what I can," said Willy. "Certainly he has some good qualities. He is as brave as a lion; and he is good-natured about giving away his own things, though he is so mischievous with other people's."

"And he is clever in his way, notwithstanding his idleness," added Margaret. "Those foolish figures that he put into my drawing were uncommonly well done, though they were provoking to us."

"You are the best girl in the world," said Willy; "and if you think Geoffrey will improve, I'll think so too; but you must own there is room for it."

Perhaps Geoffrey did improve, but it seemed slow work, faults being more easily acquired than cured; and for a long time I could perceive no difference in him. Indeed, as his next piece of mischief, concerned myself, I thought him worse than ever.

I have often wondered at the extreme dislike
which boys have to dolls. I was the most inoffen-
sive creature possible, giving myself no airs, and
interfering with nobody; yet even the gentle Willy
was indifferent to me. Edward, though he pro-
tected Rose in her patronage of me, despised me
thoroughly himself; and Geoffrey never lost an opportunity of expressing his mortal hatred to me.
I shrunk from Edward's contemptuous notice, but
I was not at all afraid of him, well knowing that
neither he nor Willy would hurt a hair of my head;
but whenever Geoffrey came into the room, terror
seized my mind. He never passed my house without making all kinds of ugly faces at me; and I felt
instinctively that nothing but the presence of the
other boys restrained him from doing me any harm
in his power.

I had hitherto never been alone with him, but
at last the fatal moment arrived. One fine after-
noon, Willy went out for a drive in his wheel-chair,
Edward insisting upon drawing it himself, and the
two girls walking on each side. Geoffrey accompanied them, intending to walk with them part of
the way, and to go on by himself when he was
tired of the slow pace of the chair. All seemed safe,
and I hoped to enjoy a few hours of uninterrupted
leisure. I always liked having my time to myself;

E

and as Rose had set me no lessons, I reposed comfortably in my arm-chair by a blazing fire of black and red cloth, from the glare of which I was sheltered by a screen. My dog sat at my side, my cat lay at my feet, and I was as happy as a doll could be.

Suddenly the silence was broken by a sound as of a turkey gabbling in the hall; presently this changed to a duck quacking on the stairs; then a cock crew on the landing-place, and a goose hissed close to the schoolroom door. I guessed but too well what these ominous sounds portended, and my heart sunk within me as the door burst open, and my dreaded enemy banged into the room.

" Why, they are not come home yet!" exclaimed he; so my talents have been wasted. I meant to have made them bid me not make every different noise. When they said, 'Don't hiss,' I would have crowed ; and when they said, ' Don't crow,' 1 would have quacked, or barked, or bellowed, or mewed, till I had gone through all the noises I know. Now I have nothing to do."

He walked to the window and looked out.

" What a stupid street it is!" said he. " If my uncle had not taken away my squirt, I would squirt at the people."

Then he yawned, and sauntered to the bookcase.

THE DOLL AND HER FRIENDS. 51

" What stupid books! I wonder any body can write them. I wish Edward had left his tools out; I should like to plane the top of the shelf. How stupid it is having nothing to do!

As he spoke, I shuddered to see him approaching my end of the room. He came nearer; he made a full stop in front of me, and looked me in the face.

" You stupid, ugly thing!" he exclaimed; " don't stare so. I hate to have a doll's eyes goggling at me."

Gladly would I have withdrawn my eyes, if possible. But they had been painted wide open, and what could I do? I never was so ashamed of them in my life; but I had no control over them, so I stared on, and he grew more indignant.

" If you don't leave off," he cried, " I'll poke out your eyes, as I did those of the ugly picture in my room. I won't be stared at."

I longed for the gift of speech to represent to him, that if he would but leave off looking at me, I should give him no offence; but alas, I was silent, and could only stare as hard as ever.

" Oh, you will, will you?" said he; " then I know what I'll do: I'll hang you."

In vain I hoped for the return of the rest of the party. I listened anxiously for every sound, but

no friendly step or voice was near, and I was completely in his power.

He began rummaging his pockets, grinning and
making faces at me all the time.   Presently he drew
forth a long piece of string, extremely dirty, looking as if it had been trailed in the mud.

" Now for it !" he exclaimed ; " now you shall
receive the reward of all your stupidity and affecta-
tion.   I do think dolls are the most affected creatures on the face of the earth."

He laid hold of me by my head, pushing my
wig on one side.   Alas for my beautiful hair, it
was disarranged for ever !   But that was a trifle
compared with what followed.   He tied one end of
his muddy string round my neck, drawing it so
tight, that I foresaw I should be marked for life,
and hung the other end to a nail in the wall.

There I dangled, while he laughed and quizzed
me, adding insult to injury.   He twisted the string
as tight as possible, and then let it whirl round and
round till it was all untwisted again.   I banged
against the wall as I spun like a top, and wished
that I could sleep like a top too.   But I was wide
awake to my misfortunes ; and each interval of
stillness, when the string was untwisted, only en-
hanced them, by showing in painful contrast the
happy home whence I had been torn.   For I was

THE DOLL IN TROUBLE. Page 52.

hung on the wall directly opposite my own house; and from my wretched nail I could distinguish every room in it. Between my twirls I saw my pretty drawing-room, with its comfortable arm-chair now vacant; and my convenient kitchen, with my respectable cook peacefully basting her perpetual mutton; I envied even my lame footman quietly seated in his chimney-corner, and felt that I had never truly valued the advantages of my home till now. Would they ever be restored to me? Should I once again be under the protection of my kind and gentle mistress, or was I Geoffrey's slave for ever?

These melancholy thoughts were interrupted by a step on the stairs. "Hallo!" cried Geoffrey, "who would have thought of their coming home just now?" and he was going to lift me down from my nail; but when the door opened, the housemaid came in alone, and he changed his mind.

"Why, Master Geoffrey," said she, "what are you doing here all alone? Some mischief, I'll be bound."

"Bow, wow, wow!" answered he, dancing and playing all sorts of antics to prevent her seeing me.

"Come," said she, "those tricks won't go down with me. The more lively you are, the more

know you've been after something you ought to
have left alone."

'Hee haw, hee haw!" said Geoffrey, twitching
her gown, and braying like a donkey.

"Well, you're speaking in your own voice at
last," said she, laughing. "But let go of my
gown, if you please; you are big enough to walk
by yourself, and I want to set the room to rights.
There's some young ladies coming to tea with Miss
Rose."

She bustled about, dusting and putting every
thing in order, and talking all the time, partly to
Geoffrey and partly to herself, about the blacks
that came in at the windows, and made a place
want dusting a dozen times a-day, when her eye
fell on my unfortunate figure, which my persecutor
had just set swinging like the pendulum of a clock.
I was a deplorable object. He had forced me
into the most awkward attitude he could invent.
My arms were turned round in their sockets,
one stretched toward the ceiling, the other at full
length on one side. I was forced to kick one leg
out in front, and the other behind; and my knees
were bent up the wrong way. My wig had fallen
off altogether from my head, and was now perched
upon my toe. I was still swinging, when Sarah
caught sight of me. She looked at me for a

moment, and then turned round, opening her eyes
at Geoffrey much wider than I had ever done.

"Why, you audacious, aggravating boy!" she
exclaimed, making a dash at him with her duster;
but he ran away laughing, and she was obliged to
finish her speech to herself.

"To think of his being so mischievous and ill-
natured! What will poor Miss Rose say? To be
sure, there is nothing boys won't do; their equals
for perverseness don't walk the earth. Though I
ought not to speak against them, while there's
Master William and Master Edward to contra-
dict me. They are boys, to be sure; but as for
that Geoffrey!" And here she shook her head in
silence, as if Geoffrey's delinquencies were beyond
the power of words to express.

She then released me; and after restoring my
limbs to their proper position, and smoothing my
discomposed dress, she laid me gently on my bed,
and placed my wig on my pillow beside me, with
many kind expressions of pity and goodwill.

Repose was indeed needful after so agitating
an adventure; and I was glad to be left quiet till
the young people came in from their walk. I com-
posed my ruffled spirits as well as I could; but I
found it impossible not to be nervous at the idea
of Rose's first seeing me in such a plight, and I

anxiously awaited her return. They came in at last, Rose, Willy, and Margaret; and after establishing Willy on his sofa, Rose's next care was to visit me. "O Willy! O Margaret!" she exclaimed, and burst into tears.

"What is the matter, my darling?" asked Margaret.

Rose could not answer; but Sarah was there to tell the story, and do ample justice to my wrongs. Yet I could not help observing, in the midst of all her indignation, the difference of her manner towards her present hearers and towards Geoffrey. She never seemed on familiar terms with Willy, much less with Margaret or Rose. She neither cut jokes nor used rough language to them, but treated them with the respect due to her master's children; though, as I well knew, she was extremely fond of them, and disliked Geoffrey, in spite of her familiarity with him.

I saw Geoffrey no more that day. Rose's young friends soon arrived, and consoled both her and me by their kind sympathy and attentions. One made an elegant cap to supply the loss of my wig; another strung a blue necklace to hide the black mark round my throat; Rose herself put me to bed, and placed a table by my bedside covered with teacups, each, she told me, containing a different medicine; and the young lady who had once brought Miss Edgeworth to dine with me, charged me to lie still and read "Rosamond" till I was quite recovered.

Next morning, as I lay contentedly performing my new part of an invalid, I heard a confidential conversation between Margaret and Geoffrey, in which I was interested.

They were alone together, and she was taking the opportunity to remonstrate with him on his unkind treatment of me.

"What was the harm?" said Geoffrey. "A doll is nothing but wood or bran, or some stupid stuff; it can't feel."

"Of course," answered Margaret, "we all know *that*. It is wasteful and mischievous to spoil a pretty toy; but I am not speaking now so much for the sake of the doll as of Rose. Rose is not made of any stupid stuff; *she* can feel. And what is more she can feel for other people as well as herself. She would never play you such an ill-natured trick."

"I should not mind it if she did," argued Geoffrey; "I am not such a baby."

"You would not mind that particular thing," answered Margaret, "because you do not care about dolls; but you would mind her interfering with *your* pleasures or injuring your property. You would think it very ill-natured, for instance, if she threw away that heap of nuts which you have hoarded like a squirrel on your shelf of the closet."

"Nuts are not nonsense like dolls," said he. "Besides, she may have as many of mine as she likes. I tried to make her eat some yesterday."

"Yes, and half choked her by poking them into her mouth, when she told you she did not want them. She cares no more for nuts than you for dolls. You would think it no kindness if she teazed you to nurse her doll."

"I should think not, indeed," answered Geoffrey, indignant at the very idea.

"Of course not. Kindness is not shewn by forcing our own pleasures down other people's throats, but by trying to promote theirs. That is really doing as we would be done by."

"But doing as we would be done by is one's *duty*," said Geoffrey.

"I fear it is a duty of which you seldom think," replied his cousin.

"Why, one can't be thinking of *duty* in those kind of things," answered he.

"Why not?" asked Margaret.

"Because they are such trifles; duties are great things."

" What sort of things do you consider to be duties ?" Margaret inquired.

"Oh, such things as letting oneself be tortured, like Regulus; or forgiving an enemy who has shot poisoned arrows at one, like Cœur de Lion."

" Well," said Margaret smiling, " such heroic duties as those do not seem likely to fall in your way just now, perhaps they never may. Our fellow-creatures are so kind to us, that we are seldom called upon to fulfil any but small duties towards them; or what you would consider such, for I cannot allow any duty to be small, especially that of doing as we would be done by. If we do not fulfil that in trifles, we shall probably never fulfil it at all. This is a serious thought, Geoffrey."

Geoffrey looked up; and as he seemed inclined to listen, Margaret continued talking to him kindly but gravely, bringing many things before his mind as duties which he had hitherto considered to be matters of indifference. But Margaret would not allow any thing to be a trifle in which one person could give pain or pleasure, trouble or relief, annoyance or comfort to another, or by which any one's own mind or habits could be either injured or improved. She maintained that there was a right and a wrong to every thing, and that right and wrong could never be trifles, whether in great things or small. By degrees the conversation turned upon matters far too solemn to be repeated by a mere plaything like myself; but I thought, as I heard her, that it might be better to be a poor wooden figure which could do neither right nor wrong, than a human being who neglected his appointed duties.

Geoffrey said little, but he shook hands with Margaret when she had finished speaking; and I noticed from that day forward a gradual improvement in his conduct. Bad habits are not cured in a minute, and he did not become all at once as gentle and considerate as Willy, nor as kind and helpful as Edward; but he put himself in the right road, and seemed in a fair way of overtaking them in due time. He at once left off *active* mischief; and if he could not avoid being occasionally troublesome, he at any rate cured himself of teazing people on purpose. And it was remarkable how many employments he found as soon as his mind was disengaged from mischief. Instead of his dawdling about all the morning calling things stupid, and saying he had nothing to do, all manner of pleasant occupations seemed to start up in his path, as if made to order for him, now that he had time to attend to them. When he relinquished the pleasure of spoiling things, he acquired the far greater pleasure of learning to make them. When Edward was no longer afraid of trusting him with his tools, it was wonderful what a carpenter he turned out. When Margaret could venture to leave drawing materials within his reach, he began to draw capitally. Good-natured Margaret gave him lessons, and said she would never wish for a better scholar. He found it was twice the pleasure to walk or play with Edward when he was thought an acquisition instead of a burden; and far more agreeable to have Rose and Willy anxious for his company than wishing to get rid of him. But the advantages were not confined to himself; the whole house shared in them: for his perpetual small annoyances had made everybody uncomfortable, whereas now, by attention to what he used to look upon as trifles, he found he had the power of contributing his part towards the happiness of his fellow-creatures, which is no trifle.

On the last day of the holidays, the young people were all assembled in the schoolroom till it was time for Edward and Geoffrey to start. While Edward was arranging various matters with Willy, I heard Geoffrey whisper to Margaret that he hoped she had forgiven him for spoiling that drawing of hers. She seemed at first really not to know what he meant; but when she recollected it, she answered with a smile, "Oh, my dear Geoffrey, I had forgiven and forgotten it long ago. Pray never think of it again yourself."

Geoffrey next went up to Rose and put a little parcel into her hands. On opening it, she found a box of very pretty bonbons in the shape of various vegetables. When she admired them, he seemed much pleased, and said that he had saved up his money to buy them, in hopes she might like them for her doll's feasts. Rose kissed and thanked him, and said she only wished he could stay and help her and her dolls to eat them. Every body took an affectionate leave of Geoffrey, and Willy said he was very sorry to lose him, and should miss him sadly.

Edward and Geoffrey returned to school, and I never saw Geoffrey again; but a constant correspondence was kept up between him and his cousins, and I often heard pleasant mention of his progress and improvement.

Time passed on; what length of time I cannot say, all seasons and their change being alike to me; but school-days and holidays succeeded one another, and our family grew older in appearance and habits. Rose gradually spent less time with me, and more with her books and music, till at last, though she still kept my house in order, she never actually played with me, unless younger children came to visit her, and *then*, indeed, I was as popular as ever. But on a little friend's one day remarking that I had worn the same gown for a month, Rose answered that she herself had the charge of her own clothes now, and that what with keeping them in order, and doing fancy-work as presents for her friends, she found no time to work for dolls.

By and by, her time for needlework was fully engaged in Geoffrey's behalf. He was going to sea; and Rose was making purses, slippers, portfolios, and every thing she could think of as likely to please him. Perhaps *her* most useful keepsake was a sailor's housewife; but many nice things were sent him from every one of the family. I saw a trunk full of presents packed and sent off. And when I recollected my first acquaintance with him, I could not but marvel over the change that had taken place, before books, drawing materials, and mathematical instruments could have been chosen as the gifts best suited to his taste.

Edward used to come home from school as merry and good-humoured as ever, and growing taller and stronger every holidays. Rose and Margaret were as flourishing as he; but poor Willy grew weaker, and thinner, and paler. Fresh springs and summers brought him no revival, but as they faded, he seemed to fade with them. He read more than ever; and his sisters were frequently occupied in reading and writing under his direction, for they were anxious to help him in his pursuits. His Papa

and Mama sometimes said he studied too hard;
and they used to sit with him, and try to amuse
him by conversation, when they wished to draw
him from his books. Doctors visited him, and pre-
scribed many remedies; and his Mama gave him all
the medicines herself, and took care that every order
was implicitly obeyed. His father carried him up
and down stairs, and waited upon him as tenderly
as even Margaret; but he grew no better with all
their care. He was always gentle and patient, but
he appeared in less good spirits than formerly. He
seemed to enjoy going out in his wheel-chair more
than any thing; but one day he observed that the
summer was fast coming to an end, and that then
he must shut himself up in his room, for that he
minded the cold more than he used.

"I wish we lived in a warmer country," said
Rose; "perhaps then you might get better."

"I do not know about *living*," replied Willy,
"England is the best country to *live* in; but I certainly should like to be out of the way of the cold
for this next winter."

"Why do not you tell Papa so?" asked Rose.

"Because I know very well he would take me
a journey directly, however inconvenient it might
be to him."

Rose said nothing more just then, but she took

the first opportunity of telling her father what had passed; and he said he was very glad indeed that she had let him know.

From that day forward something more than usual seemed in contemplation. Papa, Mama, and Margaret were constantly consulting together, and Edward, Rose, and Willy followed their example. As for me, nobody had time to bestow a look or a thought upon me; but I made myself happy by looking at and thinking of *them*.

One morning two doctors together paid Willy a long visit. After they were gone, his Papa and Mama came into his room.

" Well, my boy," his father exclaimed, in an unusually cheerful tone, " it is quite settled now; Madeira is the place, and I hope you like the plan."

" Oh, Papa," said Willy, " is it really worth while ?"

" Of course it is worth while, a hundred times over," replied his father; and we will be off in the first ship."

" The doctors strongly advise it, and we have all great hopes from it, my dear Willy," said his mother.

" Then so have I," said Willy; and, indeed, I like it extremely, and I am very grateful to you. The only thing I mind is, that you and my father should have to leave home and make a long sea-voyage, when you do not like travelling, and Papa has so much to keep him in England."

"Oh, never mind me," said his mother; I should like nothing so well as travelling, if it does you good."

"And never mind me," said his father; ". there is nothing of so much consequence to keep me in England, as your health to take me out of it."

"Besides, my dear child," said his mother, "as the change of climate is so strongly recommended for you, it becomes a duty as well as a pleasure to try it."

"So make your mind easy, my boy," added his father; "and I will go and take our passage for Madeira."

The father left the room, and the mother remained conversing with her sick child, whose spirits were unusually excited. I scarcely knew him again. He was generally slow and quiet, and rather desponding about himself; but he now thought he should certainly get well, and was so eager and anxious to start without delay, that his mother had some difficulty in reconciling him to the idea that no ship would sail till next month. She also took great pains to impress upon him the duty of resignation, in case the attempt should fail, after all, in restoring his health ; and she finally left him, not less hopeful, but more calm and contented with whatever might befall him.

And now began the preparations for the voyage. There was no time to spare, considering all that had to be done. Everybody was at work; and though poor Willy himself could not do much to help, he thought of nothing else. His common books and drawings were changed for maps and voyages ; the track to Madeira was looked up by him and Rose every day, and sometimes two or three times in the day, and every book consulted that contained the least reference to the Madeira Isles.

Edward was an indefatigable packer. He was not to be one of the travellers, as his father did not choose to interrupt his school-education ; but no one was more active than he in forwarding the preparations for the voyage, and no one more sanguine about its results.

" We shall have Willy back," he would say, " turned into a fine strong fellow, as good a cricketer as Geoffrey or I, and a better scholar than either of us."

Margaret and Rose were to go; and Rose's young friends all came to take leave of her, and talk over the plan, and find Madeira in the map, and look at views of the island, which had been given to Willy. And a sailor-friend who had been all over the world, used to come and describe Madeira as one of the most beautiful of all the beautiful places he had visited, and tell of its blue sea, fresh and bright, without storms; its high mountains, neither barren nor bleak : and its climate, so warm and soft, that Willy might sit out all day in the beautiful gardens, under hedges of fragrant geraniums. And when Willy talked of enjoying the gardens while his stronger sisters were climbing the hills, there was more to be told of cradles borne upon men's shoulders, in which Willy could be carried to the top of the highest hills as easily as his sisters on their mountain ponies.

And now the packing was all finished, and the luggage sent on board, and every body was anxious to follow it; for the ship was reported as quite comfortable, and the house was decidedly the reverse. Margaret and her father had been on board to arrange the cabins, accompanied by their sailor-friend, who professed to know how to fit up a berth better than any body. He had caused all the furniture to be fastened, or, as he called it, *cleated* to the floor, that it might not roll about in rough weather. The books were secured in the shelves by bars, and swinging tables hung from the ceilings. Willy's couch was in the most airy and

convenient place at the stern cabin window, and
there was an easy chair for him when he should
be able to come out on deck. The ship was said
to be in perfect order, whereas the house was in
the utmost confusion and desolation : the carpets
rolled up, the pictures taken down, the mirrors
covered with muslin, the furniture and bookcases
with canvas; not a vestige left of former habits
and occupations, except me and my little mansion.
But in the midst of all the bustle, I was as calm
and collected as if nothing had happened. I sat
quietly in my arm-chair, staring composedly at all
that went on, contented and happy, though appa-
rently forgotten by every body. Indeed, such was
my placid, patient disposition, that I do not believe
I should have uttered a sound or moved a muscle if
the whole of London had fallen about my little ears.

I did certainly sometimes wish to know what
was to become of me, and at last that information
was given me.

The night before they sailed, Rose busied herself
with Sarah in packing up my house and furniture,
which were to be sent to a little girl who had long
considered it her greatest treat to play with them.
But Rose did not pack me up with my goods and
chattels.

"My poor old Seraphina," said she, as she

removed me from my arm-chair, "you and I have passed many a happy day together, and I do not like to throw you away as mere rubbish ; but the new mistress of your house has already more dolls than she knows what to do with. You are no great beauty now, but I wish I knew any child who would care for you."

"If you please to give her to me, Miss Rose," said Sarah, "my little niece, that your Mama is so kind as to put to school, would thank you kindly, and think her the greatest of beauties."

"Oh, then, take her by all means, Sarah," replied Rose : "and here is a little trunk to keep her clothes in. I remember I used to be very fond of that trunk; so I dare say your little Susan will like it, though it is not quite new."

"That she will, and many thanks to you, Miss. Susan will be as delighted with it now, as you were a year or two ago."

So they wrapped me up in paper, and Rose having given me a farewell kiss, which I would have returned if I could, Sarah put me and my trunk both into her great pocket ; and on the same day that my old friends embarked for their distant voyage, I was carried to my new home.

CHAPTER III.

AND now began a third stage of my existence, and
a fresh variety of life.

I at first feared that I should have great difficulty in reconciling myself to the change; and my
reflections in Sarah's dark pocket were of the most
gloomy cast. I dreaded poverty and neglect. How
should I, accustomed to the refinements of polished
life and the pleasures of cultivated society, endure
to be tossed about with no home of my own, and
perhaps no one who really cared for me! I knew
that I was not in my first bloom, and it seemed un-
likely that a new acquaintance should feel towards
me like my old friend Rose, who had so long known
my value. Perhaps I might be despised; perhaps
allowed to go ragged, perhaps even dirty! My
spirits sunk, and had I been human, I should have
wept.

But cheerful voices aroused me from this melancholy reverie, and I found myself restored to the
pleasant light in the hands of a goodhumoured-look-
ing little girl, whose reception of me soon banished
my fears. For, although altered since the days of

my introduction to the world in the bazaar, so that
my beauty was not quite what it had been, I still
retained charms enough to make me a valuable acquisition to a child who had not much choice of toys;
and my disposition and manners were as amiable
and pleasing as ever.   My new mistress and I
soon loved each other dearly; and in her family
I learned that people might be equally happy and
contented under very different outward circumstances.

Nothing could well be more unlike my former
home than that to which I was now introduced.
Susan, my little mistress, was a child of about the
same age as Rose when she first bought me; but
Susan had no money to spend in toys, and very
little time to play with them, though she enjoyed
them as much as Rose herself.   She gave me a
hearty welcome; and though she could offer me no
furnished house, with its elegancies and comforts,
she assigned me the best place in her power—the
corner of a shelf on which she kept her books, slate,
needlework, and inkstand.   And there I lived, sitting on my trunk, and observing human life from a
new point of view. And though my dignity might
appear lowered in the eyes of the unthinking, I felt
that the respectability of my character was really
in no way diminished; for I was able to fulfil the

great object of my existence as well as ever, by giving innocent pleasure, and being useful in my humble way.

No other dolls now visited me; but I was not deprived of the enjoyments of inanimate society, for I soon struck up an intimate acquaintance with an excellent Pen in the inkstand by my side, and we passed our leisure hours very pleasantly in communicating to each other our past adventures. His knowledge of life was limited, having resided in that inkstand, and performed all the writing of the family, ever since he was a quill. But his experience was wise and virtuous; and he could bear witness to many an industrious effort at improvement, in which he had been the willing instrument; and to many a hard struggle for honesty and independence, which figures of his writing had recorded. I liked to watch the good Pen at his work when the father of the family spent an hour in the evening in teaching Susan and her brothers to write; or when the careful mother took him in hand to help her in balancing her accounts, and ascertaining that she owed no one a penny, before she ventured upon any new purchase. Then my worthy friend was in his glory; and it was delightful to see how he enjoyed his work. He had but one fault, which was a slight tendency to splutter; and as he was obliged to keep that under restraint while engaged in writing, he made himself amends by a little praise of himself when relating his exploits to a sympathising friend like myself. On his return with the inkstand to the corner of my shelf, he could not resist sometimes boasting when he had not made a single blot; or confessing to me, in perfect confidence, how much the thinness of Susan's upstrokes, or the thickness of her downstrokes, was owing to the clearness of his slit or the fineness of his nib.

The family of which we made part lived frugally and worked hard : but they were healthy and happy. The father with his boys went out early in the morning to the daily labour by which they maintained the family. The mother remained at home, to take care of the baby and do the work of the house. She was the neatest and most careful person I ever saw, and she brought up her daughter Susan to be as notable as herself.

Susan was an industrious little girl, and in her childish way worked almost as hard as her mother. She helped to sweep the house, and nurse the baby, and mend the clothes, and was as busy as a bee. But she was always tidy; and though her clothes were often old and shabby, I never saw them dirty or ragged. Indeed, I must own that, in point of *neatness*, Susan was even superior to my old friend

Rose. Rose would break her strings, or lose her buttons, or leave holes in her gloves, till reproved by her mama for untidiness : but Susan never forgot that "a stitch in time saves nine," and the stitch was never wanting.

She used to go to school for some hours every day : and I should have liked to go with her, and help her in her studies, especially when I found that she was learning the multiplication-table, and I remembered how useful I had been to Rose in that very lesson ; but dolls were not allowed at school, and I was obliged to wait patiently for Susan's company till she had finished all her business, both at school and at home.

She had so little time to bestow upon me, that at first I began to fear that I should be of no use to her. The suspicion was terrible ; for the wish to be useful has been the great idea of my life. It was my earliest hope, and it will be my latest pleasure. I could be happy under almost any change of circumstances ; but as long as a splinter of me remains, I should never be able to reconcile myself to the degradation of thinking that I had been *of no use.*

But I soon found I was in no danger of what I so much dreaded. In fact, I seemed likely to be even more useful to Susan than to Rose. Before I

had been long in the house, she said one evening
that she had an hour to spare, and that she would
make me some clothes.

"Well and good," answered her mother; "only
be sure to put your best work in them. If you
mind your work, the doll will be of great use to
you, and you can play without wasting your time."

This was good hearing for Susan and me, and
she spent most of her leisure in working for me.
While she was thus employed, I came down from
my shelf, and was treated with as much consideration as when Rose and her companions waited at
my table.

A great change took place in my wardrobe.
Rose had always dressed me in gay silks and satins,
without much regard to under-clothing; for, she
said, as my gowns must be sewn on, what did any
petticoats signify? So she sewed me up, and I
looked very smart; and if there happened to be any
unseemly cobbling, she hid it with beads or span-
gles.   Once I remember a very long stitch baffled
all her contrivances, and she said I must pretend it
was a new-fashioned sort of embroidery.

But Susan scorned all *make-shifts.*   Nothing
could have been more unfounded than my fears of
becoming ragged or dirty.   My attire was plain and
suited to my station, but most scrupulously finished.

She saw no reason why my clothes should not be made to take off and on, as well as if I had been a doll three feet high. So I had my plain gingham gowns with strings and buttons; and my shifts and petticoats run and felled, gathered and whipped, hemmed and stitched, like any lady's; and every thing was neatly marked with my initial S. But what Susan and I were most particularly proud of, was a pair of stays. They were a long time in hand, for the fitting them was a most difficult job; but when finished, they were such curiosities of needlework, that Susan's neat mother herself used to show off the stitching and the eyelet-holes to every friend that came to see her.

Among them, Sarah the housemaid, who was sister to Susan's father, often called in to ask after us all. She was left in charge of the house where my former friends had lived, and they sometimes sent her commissions to execute for them. Then she was sure to come and bring us news of *the family*, as she always called Rose and her relations. Sometimes she told us that Master William was a little better; sometimes that she heard Miss Rose was very much grown: she had generally something to tell that we were all glad to hear. One evening, soon after my apparel was quite completed, I was sitting on my trunk, as pleased with myself as Susan was with me, when Sarah's head peeped in at the door.

"Good evening to you all," said she; " I thought as I went by, you would like to hear that I have a letter from the family, and all's well. I have got a pretty little job to do for master Willy. He is to have a set of new shirts sent out directly, made of very fine thin calico, because his own are too thick. See, here is the stuff I have been buying for them."

" It is beautiful calico, to be sure," said Susan's mother; " but such fine stuff as that will want very neat work. I am afraid you will hardly be able to make them yourself."

" Why, no," answered Sarah, smiling and shaking her head. " I am sorry to say, *there* comes in my old trouble, not having learned to work neatly when I was young. Take warning by me, Susan, and mind your needlework now-a-days. If I could work as neatly as your mother, my mistress would have made me lady's maid and housekeeper by this time. But I could not learn any but rough work, more's the pity: so I say again, take warning by *me*, little niece; take pattern by your mother."

Susan looked at me and smiled, as much as to say, "I have taken pattern by her"; but she had not time to answer, for Sarah continued, addressing the mother:

" How I wish you could have time to do this job! for it would bring you in a pretty penny, and I know my mistress would be pleased with your work ; but they are to be done very quickly, in time for the next ship, and I do not see that you *could* get through them with only one pair of hands."

"We have two pair of hands," cried Susan; " here are mine."

" Ah, but what can they do ?" asked Sarah, "and how can they do it ? It is not enough to have four fingers and a thumb. Hands must be handy."

"And so they are," answered Susan's mother. " See whether any hands could do neater work than that." And she pointed me out to Sarah.

Sarah took me up, and turned me from side to side. Then she looked at 'my hems, then at my seams, then at my gathers, while I felt truly proud and happy, conscious that not a long stitch could be found in either.

" Well to be sure !" exclaimed she, after examining me all over; " do you mean that all that is really Susan's own work ?"

" Every stitch of it" replied the mother; " and I think better need not be put into any shirt, though Master William does deserve the best of every thing."

" You never said a truer word, neither for Master William nor for little Susan," replied Sarah ; " and I wish you joy, Susan, of being able to help your mother so nicely, for now I can leave you the job to do between you."

She then told them what was to be the payment for the work, which was a matter I did not myself understand, though I could see that it gave them great satisfaction.

The money came at a most convenient time, to help in fitting out Susan's brother Robert for a place which had been offered to him in the country. It was an excellent place ; but there were several things, as his mother well knew, that poor Robert wanted at starting, but would not mention for fear his parents should distress themselves to obtain them for him. Both father and mother had been saving for the purpose, without saying any thing about it to Robert ; but they almost despaired of obtaining more than half the things they wanted, till this little sum of money came into their hands so opportunely.

The father was in the secret, but Robert could scarcely believe his eyes, when one evening his mother and Susan laid on the table before him, one by one, all the useful articles he wished to possess. At first he seemed almost more vexed than pleased, for he thought of the saving and the slaving that his mother must have gone through to gain them; but when she told him how much of them was due to his little sister's neatness and industry, and how easy the work had been when shared between them, he was as much pleased as Susan herself.

We were all very happy that evening, including even the humble friends on the shelf; for I sat on my trunk, and related to the Pen how useful I had been in teaching Susan to work; and the worthy Pen stood bolt upright in his inkstand, and confided to me with honest pride, that Robert had been chosen to his situation on account of his excellent writing.

Time passed on, and I suppose we all grew older, as I noticed from time to time various changes that seemed to proceed from that cause. The baby, for instance, though still going by the name of "Baby," had become a strong able-bodied child, running alone, and very difficult to keep out of mischief. The most effectual way of keeping her quiet was to place me in her hands, when she would sit on the floor nursing me by the hour together, while her mother and sister were at work.

Susan was become a tall strong girl, more notable than ever, and, like Rose before her, she gradually bestowed less attention on me; so that I was beginning to feel myself neglected, till on a certain

G

birthday of her little sister, she declared her intention of making me over altogether to the baby-sister
for a birthday present. Then I once more rose into
importance, and found powers which I thought de-
clining, still undiminished. The baby gave a scream
of delight when I was placed in her hand as her
own. Till then she had only possessed one toy in
the world, an old wooden horse, in comparison
with which I seemed in the full bloom of youth and
beauty. This horse, which she called JACK, had
lost not merely the ornaments of mane and tail,
but his head, one fore and one hind leg; so that
nothing remained of the once noble quadruped but
a barrel with the paint scratched off, rather in-
securely perched upon a stand with wheels. But
he was a faithful animal, and did his work to the
last. The baby used to tie me on to his barrel,
and Jack and I were drawn round and round the
kitchen with as much satisfaction to our mistress,
as in the days when I shone forth in my gilt coach
with its four prancing piebalds.

But the baby's treatment of me, though grati-
fying from its cordiality, had a roughness and want
of ceremony that affected my enfeebled frame. I
could not conceal from myself that the infirmities
I had observed in other dolls were gradually gaining
ground upon me. Nobody ever said a harsh word

to me, or dropped a hint of my being less pretty
than ever, and the baby called me "Beauty,
beauty," twenty times a day; but still I knew
very well that not only had my rosy colour and
fine hair disappeared, but I had lost the whole of
one leg and half of the other, and the lower joints of
both my arms. In fact, as my worthy friend the Pen
observed, both he and I were reduced to stumps.

The progress of decay caused me no regret, for
I felt that I had done my work, and might now
gracefully retire from public life, and resign my
place to newer dolls. But though contented with
my lot, I had still one anxious wish ungratified.
The thought occupied my mind incessantly; and
the more I dwelt upon it, the stronger grew the
hope that I might have a chance of seeing my old
first friends once more. This was now my only remaining care.

News came from them from time to time. Sarah
brought word that Master William was better;
that they had left Madeira, and gone travelling
about elsewhere. Then that the father had been
in England upon business, and gone back again;
that Mr. Edward had been over to foreign parts
one summer holidays to see his family, and on his
return had come to give her an account of them.

Sarah was always very bustling when she had

any news to bring of the family, but one day she called on us in even more flurry than usual. She was quite out of breath with eagerness.

"Sit down and rest a minute before you begin to speak," said her quiet sister-in-law. "There must be some great news abroad. It seems almost too much for you."

Susan nodded, and began to unpack a great parcel she had brought with her.

"It don't seem bad news, to judge by your face," said the other; for now that Sarah had recovered breath, her smiles succeeded one another so fast, that she seemed to think words superfluous.

"I guess, I guess!" cried Susan. "They are coming home."

"They are, indeed," answered Sarah at last; "they are coming home as fast as steam-engines can bring them: and here is work more than enough for you and mother till they come. Miss Margaret is going to be married, and you are to make the wedding-clothes."

So saying, she finished unpacking her parcel, and produced various fine materials which required Susan's neatest work.

"These are for you to begin with," said she, "but there is more coming." She then read a letter from the ladies with directions about the needlework, to which Susan and her mother listened with great attention. Then Sarah jumped up, saying she must not let the grass grow under her feet, for she had plenty to do. The whole house was to be got ready; and she would not have a thing out of its place, nor a speck of dust to be found, for any money.

Susan and her mother lost no time either; their needles never seemed to stop: and I sat on the baby's lap watching them, and enjoying the happy anticipation that my last wish would soon be accomplished.

But though Susan was as industrious as a girl could be, and just now wished to work harder than ever, she was not doomed to "all work and no play;" for her father took care that his children should enjoy themselves at proper times. In summer evenings, after he came home from his work, they used often to go out all together for a walk in the nearest park, when he and his wife would rest under the trees, and read over Robert's last letter, while the children amused themselves. Very much we all enjoyed it, for even I was seldom left behind. Susan would please the baby by dressing me in my best clothes for the walk; and the good-natured father would laugh merrily at us, and remark how much good the fresh air did me. We were all very happy; and when my thoughts travelled to other scenes and times, I sometimes wondered whether my former friends enjoyed themselves as much in their southern gardens, as this honest family in their English fields.

Our needlework was finished and sent to Sarah's care to await Margaret's arrival, for which we were very anxious.

On returning home one evening after our walk, we passed, as we often did, through the street in which I had formerly lived. Susan was leading her little sister, who, on her part, clutched me in a way very unlike the gentleness which Susan bestowed upon her. On arriving at the well-known house, we saw Sarah standing at the area-gate. We stopped to speak to her.

"When are they expected?" asked Susan's mother.

"They may be here any minute," answered Sarah: "Mr. Edward has just brought the news."

The street-door now opened, and two gentlemen came out and stood on the steps. One was a tall fine-looking boy, grown almost into a young man; but I could not mistake the open good-humoured countenance of my old friend Edward. The other was older, and I recognised him as the traveller who used to describe Madeira to Willy.

They did not notice us, for we stood back so as not to intrude, and their minds were evidently fully occupied with the expected meeting.

" We all gazed intently down the street, every voice hushed in eager interest. Even my own little mistress, usually the noisiest of her tribe, was silent as myself. It was a quiet street and a quiet time, and the roll of the distant carriages would scarcely have seemed to break the silence, had it not been for our intense watching, and hoping that the sound of every wheel would draw nearer. We waited long, and were more than once disappointed by carriages passing us and disappearing at the end of the street. Edward and his friend walked up and down, east and west, north and south, in hopes of descrying the travellers in the remotest distance. But after each unavailing walk, they took up their post again on the steps.

At last a travelling carriage laden with luggage turned the nearest corner, rolled towards us, and stopped at the house. The two gentlemen rushed down the steps, flung open the carriage-door, and for some moments all was hurry and agitation, and I could distinguish nothing.

I much feared that I should now be obliged to go home without actually seeing my friends, for they had passed so quickly from the carriage to the house, and there had been so much confusion and excitement during those few seconds, that my transient glance scarcely allowed me to know one from another; but in course of time Sarah came out again, and asked Susan's father to help in unloading the carriage, desiring us to sit meanwhile in the housekeeper's room. So we waited till the business was finished, when, to my great joy, we were summoned to the sitting-room, and I had the happiness of seeing all the family once more assembled.

I was delighted to find how much less they were altered than I. I had been half afraid that I might see one without a leg, another without an arm, according to the dilapidations which had taken place in my own frame; but, strange to say, their sensitive bodies, which felt every change of weather, shrunk from a rough touch, and bled at the scratch of a pin, had outlasted mine, though insensible to pain or sickness. There stood the father, scarcely altered; his hair perhaps a little more grey, but his eyes as quick and bright as ever. And there was the mother, still grave and gentle, but looking less sad and careworn than in the days of Willy's constant illness. And there was, first in interest to me, my dear Mistress, Rose, as tall as Margaret, and as handsome as Edward. I could not imagine her condescending to play with me now.

Margaret looked just as in former times, good and graceful; but she stood a little apart with the traveller-friend by her side, and I heard Rose whisper to Susan that the wedding was to take place in a fortnight. They were only waiting for Geoffrey to arrive. His ship was daily expected, and they all wished him to be present.

And Willy, for whose sake the long journey had been made, how was he? Were all their hopes realised? Edward shook his head when Susan's mother asked that question; but Willy was there to answer it himself. He was standing by the window, leaning on a stick, it is true, but yet able to stand. As he walked across the room, I saw that he limped slightly, but could move about where he pleased. He still looked thin and pale, but the former expression of suffering and distress had disappeared, and his countenance was as cheerful as his manner. I could see that he was very much better, though not in robust health like Edward. He thanked Susan's mother for her kind inquiries, and said that, though he had not become all that his sanguine brother hoped, he had gained health more than enough to satisfy himself; that he was most thankful for his present comfort and independence; and that if he was not quite so strong as other people, he hoped he should at any rate make a good use of the strength that was allowed him. Turning to Edward, who still looked disappointed, he continued: "Who could have ventured to hope, Edward, three years ago, that you and I should now be going to college together?" And then even Edward smiled and seemed content.

As we turned to leave the room, Susan and her little sister lingered for a moment behind the others, and the child held me up towards Rose. Rose started, and exclaimed, "Is it possible? It really *is* my poor old Seraphina. Who would have thought of her being still in existence? What a good, usefull doll she has been! I really must give her a kiss once more for old friendship's sake."

So saying, she kissed both me and the baby, and we left the house.

And now there remains but little more for me to relate. My history and my existence are fast drawing to an end; my last wish has been gratified by my meeting with Rose, and my first hope realised by her praise of my usefulness. She has since given the baby a new doll, and I am finally laid on the shelf, to enjoy, in company with my respected friend the Pen, a tranquil old age. When he, like myself, was released from active work, and replaced by one of Mordan's patent steel, he kindly offered to employ his remaining leisure in writing from my dictation, and it is in compliance with his advice that I have thus ventured to record my experience.

That experience has served to teach me that, as all inanimate things have some destined use, so all rational creatures have some appointed duties, and are happy and well employed while fulfilling them.

With this reflection, I bid a grateful farewell to those young patrons of my race who have kindly taken an interest in my memoirs, contentedly awaiting the time when the small remnant of my frame shall be reduced to dust, and my quiet existence sunk into a still more profound repose.

THE END.

WERTHEIMER AND CO., PRINTERS, CIRCUS PLACE.